Published in 2024 by FeedARead.com Publis

First Edition

A CIP catalogue record for this title is available from the British Library.

Acknowledgements

Many thanks to Dave Morgan of Third Sector Projects who was the judge on this edition and proved to be accessible and diligent in his task!
Also thanks to Forever Manchester and Bolton CVS who continued to offer support.
Congratulations to those within who won the various competition prizes and lastly thank you everyone for your valid participation and contribution.

Dedication

In memory of Paul Blackburn, friend, poet, writer and songster who worked with us over many years and made a huge contribution to the written and spoken word across North West England.

Disclaimer

ENVIRONMENT

CREATIVE MIND
AN ANTHOLOGY
OF POETRY AND PROSE

INTRODUCTION

How does the environment grab you as a topic? We had a luke-warm response when the feelers were put out. People seem to tire of the repetition of the subject and maybe shy away from the negativity that often accompanies it. The world is NOT coming to an end. At least these writings try to be more uplifting and relaxing and avoid the debacle of gloom, doom, stagnation and the grim reaper.
A variety of writings examines different landscapes, industrial coal mining areas, an urban zone, natural places like caves, hedgerows, trees, seas and woods amidst the country's splendor. Certain pieces carry a strong sense of eco-contemplation, peace and adaptability either by personal activity or the implementation of improvements or technology. Others point the way to disturbance or upheaval in the form of volcanoes or wildfires and the impact of the fashion industry with its excess, contamination, waste and exploitation of native people. The environment is everywhere as highlighted in these pages, something of a daily pleasure, leisure, impact and reckoning. Presentations are covered in a personal or practical, adventurous, insightful, spiritual historical or documentary way, each adding a special understanding of the world around in all its manifest forms.
A good sense of understanding and adjustment illustrates there is no need for retreat or surrender. It is interesting the varied approaches the writers have all taken in their task and should be congratulated for sticking to the narrative with propaganda thankfully in short supply. Starting with a near homage to Ginsberg, the journey moves swiftly on with an eco-twist as the magic of a new environmental space can evolve. Things only fall apart relatively speaking as a fresh land provides fortitude and plentitude. There is reflection and animation with a feeling for the beauty of the earth with the imagination stimulated to touch new depths. Nature can still conjure up the romance in the same way as Keats, Wordsworth and Walt Whitman had it – such a tour de force is life on earth!
For some the concentration on the environment brings out their 'other' side, the transcendent and deeply felt view of the world that there is a need to embrace.

If you wish to engage with us in creative writing workshops and/or anthologies please contact the editor at: h.prescott@yahoo.co.uk or https://www.creative-mind-co.uk

Editor: Helen Prescott

CONTENTS

REGENERATION

Sue Gerrard

The Mining Generation:
I have seen the best of nature destroyed by sunken
hollow pits hewn out of our generous land. Deep black
shafts stretching to hell and back where man
and machine hacked to disembowel our earth,
turning paradise into petrified ground all around.
Dynamite blasting away 'England's green and pleasant land'
Leaving dark satanic slag heaps, like the devil's soulless angels,
standing guard over Dante's inferno; silently applauding
as the earth spews forth its black treasure.
Worth this measure of destruction?

I have seen black abandoned mines litter the once
beautiful horizon. Bitter churned land is home to
discarded, unwanted earth while pits are an
underground labyrinth of hopelessness where
gas seeps, water erodes the weeping walls and
where men and boys died.

The New Generation:
I now see the miracle of earth's redemption;
reclaimed, returned, revisited and rejoice at
the rebirth all around. Families stroll through
tall, leafy forests tickled by sapling branches,
trees no longer wheeze but sway in fresh breeze.
They catch whispers and laughter for eternity.
This is now our land of celebration as we return
what we stole so long ago. Nature forgives.
Regeneration begins as weaving rivers guide
our steps to our canopy of unpolluted sky
and pure air fills our lungs as birds fly by.

I now see the joy of generations looking to a
resurgence of greenness, of intriguing
wetlands and flashes and evasive reed birds
rarely seen but always heard.

I now see generations of families embraced
by beauty, enchanted by the wonder
of what is here. Ours to take in, ours to
take home to treasure in our memories forever then
to pass on, like a baton, to the next generation.
Our brave new world is here and
will live on and on and on…

THE SEA *SWIMBLE

Maggie Fawcett

**swimble – to enjoy an aimless immersion in water*

They gathered at twilight by the shuttered arcade,
Wrapped in tight skins, over mature hearts.
Herded against unguarded stares,
Crossed a cobbled beach to the water's edge.
Urged on with oaths and warmed words,
They side stepped through foaming surf.
Alone dipped –dived beneath the waves,
Emerged together, icicle flushed.
Jumped backwards over white-topped breakers.
Arms raised, they laughed, wild.

Out in the deep quiet calm,
They talked in hushed whispers,
Spoke of hopes and dreams.
Announced of births and deaths,
Described family scandals.
Watched and watched over with mindful care,
Hugged tow floats with limbs unseen,
And rested tired heads on the luminescent pillows. Floated, cradle rocked,
Effortlessly adrift.

Lifted by an uneasy swell,
Awakened limbs pushed and pulled,
Worked landward against a relentless force.
Blown like spindrift, beached on shift-sand.
Earth bound, they breathed deep,
And walked proudly tall past now envious eyes.
Wrapped against the bitter chill,
They sipped from flasks, shared sweet cake,
And shiver-smiled,
Returned alive.

THIS IS MY CHURCH

Peter Smith

This is my temple, this is my church
As I walk in this forest through God's great works
Here is my synagogue, here is my mosque
In a place which I found when I felt lost

No bars or doors in this sacred space
Somewhere to worship whatever your faith
So come and pay homage when your soul feels down
On a path that might take you to the higher ground

I pray at this bench though it could be a pew
As I gaze at the leaves where the sun shines through
Stained glass windows they might well be
Rather than the foliage on a sycamore tree

Why raise the roof when these trees have their boughs?
Who needs a font when this stream gently flows?
So keep all those relics, that silver and gold
With the snowdrops and daffodils our riches will grow

If the bluebells could ring they would ring out rejoice
As these woodlands vibrate with one unified voice
Listen to the choirs as springtime blooms
Where the birds sing the words and the bees hum the tunes

Blow incense blow in this garden untamed
Grow spirit grow in this Eden reclaimed
In this shelter, this haven, this heaven on earth
For this is my temple, for this is my church

SEA GRASS

Celia Hinton

I am the waves of wild sea savannah,
I live in the shallows,
soak up the sunlight,
secretly shelter cuttlefish, crab and seahorse.
sequestering more carbon
than rainforest or wetland,
I am the health of ocean,
shield against sea's acidity,
safeguard from storm surge.
I nurture turtle and dugong,
coral reef and mangrove,
nurse fish, filter pollutants,
anchor the ground in these liminal strands.

We've lost 92% of sea grass meadows around the UK from trawler damage in the last 100 years.
However, there is an experimental scientific regeneration programme in the Solent and Dale in Pembrokeshire, harvesting seeds and planting them in small hessian bags on the neritic sea floor.

PEMBROKESHIRE

Celia Hinton

Here, where the earth meets the sea
at the edge of the world,
Is a thin, liminal place.

It's a land of sea fret and blown spume,
holy wells and sacred springs,
Streams rushing down to the ocean,
hidden coves where the west wind funnels
up narrow valleys into the hinterland.

In the woods, red campion petals and ragged robin glow

among the secret moon faces of white stitchwort

a lone cuckoo calls from beyond the hill.

On the southern cliffs clumps of pink thrift blaze
amid sunburst gorse and blue fields of squat squill;
an ancient stone circle gazes blindly out to sea,,
choughs swoop from the black slicked rocks
where the gulls scream.
my heart sings in this thin place,
this land of St Dafydd.

CHAFFINCH
Celia Hinton

Charming, chittering chaffinch,
Hopping up, mopping up scattered seeds,
Arable winter stubble-feeder,
Florid February cadence-singer,
Foot-over-shoulder head scratcher.
Inimitable
Not-so-many-these-days
Crab apple core-pip picking
Hungry hedge-nester.

BORN TOO SOON
Annette Heys

Blue sky and bright orange sunbeams glance
through jagged white topped branches
to contradict the icy landscape.
Still, a fresh day is welcome after
Christmas spent opening presents, drinking
wine and making merry because it is, Christmas.

Frost laden fields lie ahead, their way gained
through deep rugged tracks, lace edged and
lined with three pronged prints where birds sought water.
I add my mark; delve a boot sharp down to hear the
sound of cracking, crunching ice.

Stopping at the kissing gate, I rest to survey a
frozen land of stiff hedgerows, sloping fields where
fat black comma crows make distinct against a
bland backdrop. Blue, black and white make a
display of perfect picture symmetry, its beauty
freeze framed with other such ghost white memories.

The shortest day now past invokes the promise of spring
when bud and blade break out and charge this barren
earth once more with renewed fecundity.

With lightened step, I pass between the wooden frame
to a field where sheep scatter en mass as if breeze blown.
But there stands one, alone, unmoved by my trespass,
whose dreadful bleating scars the scene. Closer, and its
distress is clear – two small white bodies hug the frozen
grass and my day is shattered like broken ice.

Letter No. 1 **On the 'Environment'**
Nicole Bartos

My friend, without implanting oneself on the paths of nature whether out in the wild or in the cityscape parks and meadows, the visual perception which one retains the information about the environment, it is rather grey and heavy; one may forget to look up to the sky and the analytics, the analytical perception of the elements of this Universe, wood, water.., are faded away.

Much notice that green areas around cities are reduced and with it harmony and silence, nature's colours, birds, all wild life diminish. Buildings and ever growing traffic expand beyond control, encaging us, as if in a "city prison" of the sort, where nature is a thin slice and the parks left, are the only reminiscent green components, images of Nature, close at hand.

We get great pleasure from walks. Walks around rivers... Promenades around lakes and woods... We all do, when we decide to reach out to them and, tune back in the Nature's pure resonance. Do we still design and build parks and lakes, reservoirs of life and water?

My friend, I share with you statements, thoughts and questions. Are you aware of your closest beautiful green spots, in and around your location? Can you reach them daily? Can you fill them with your care and memories; can you obtain the fragrance from the morning breeze and the taste of the mist on the lake; the fine morning dew on the grass? Does it make you feel full of hope and energised? Does your favourite tree still stands, today? Do your favourite birds still sing? Does your favourite bench still awaiting you, to pause and does your rush still turns into contemplation? Does your friend still walk with you, on your favourite path and in your favourite spots?

We may take it all for granted until one day the tree falls, the bird dies, vanishes out of site never to return; the bench crumbles away, the friend grows old and frail, and we limit ourselves to a slow walk to the shop and back home...

Love, and rest in your environment, your neighbourhood, make it ever new and fresh, ever clean and colourful in diversity, let's make it special and nourishing for all, soulful and healing, by allowing it's nature to be, to live, procreate, allowing it to be near.

Let's walk, breathe, smile, plant our gardens of hopes and joy, our flowers. Our garden sweet peas should burst of sweet fragrance and love.
I'll see you in my walks. Good bye, see you soon, my friend!

***Letter No. 2* on the 'Emptiness'**
"Some Emptiness"

Lakes gather in valleys...Lakes gather from rain and rivulets, streams that flow from downhill, from mountains or through manmade water downs.
In the empty sky, clouds and rainbows come and go... In the vast wilderness, trees grow. Forests, woods expand, extend as far as the emptiness lasts, where the ground is good, rich and unpolluted. In the vastness of the sea or oceans, fish varieties richly populate the waters.
... In caves, gems and crystals form, around water flow trajectories; long hidden dry paths under the mountain rock or formations. I had listened once to a mesmerising acoustic of a string concert in an amazing cave, near Serb-Croat border.
In an empty garden pot some spring bulbs grow, planted in fresh compost. They are coming out beautifully.
In an empty cup tea is served; in a plastic or glass bottle mineral water is stored and sold; in an empty house, somebody moves in and fills it up with personality, laughter, emotions of love, sorrow; furniture, books and memories are stocked up amongst the empty walls. In an empty stomach, hunger shouts and growls..
In emptiness, silence arises; in an empty mind, spirit leads the way, in the empty gloves, your hands fit and are warmed up;
...in a great hat your beautiful head and hair locks hide.
In an empty day, your everything rolls in and happens suddenly; in an empty shop, food and flowers arrive and are sold from; in an empty pocket, your hands warm up and relax; and again, air fills up the empty space, it takes its' mould, it's shape...
In a vast Universe, the planets, stars, our world exist.
Everything seems to be lying in and around emptiness or, is being determined by it?
In an empty quiet moment, creativity is born and soul rests feeling at peace. Healing is there, in emptiness.

Like an empty tin, filled with tea bags or biscuits, so my thoughts, like books on a shelf line up and float in emptiness of my mind;
Where emptiness is, a deep breath follows you and beautiful sound or song is born. In the empty resonance box there is *'re-so-nan-ce'*, and the strings of my harp, sound louder in an empty room, and thanks to its' resonance box. In the empty, open mouth, sound follows and words are uttered; songs and chants, streaming out in the Universe...
In the empty coat, my body walks in, inhabits it...
In the empty nest, the wren moved in. And, on the empty lake, two swans moved in, together...
From the empty lit light bulb, light spreads out and irrigates the room.
Through your eye socket your eyes and your soul see the world...
On the empty paper you write your thoughts, stories; in an empty bag you take home some pears, magazines... you name it.
So, emptiness is necessary, is always giving birth to new things and relationships, to new combinations, and determines new things. We empty something so later it can be filled up again.
In the empty drawer, my dreams, calculations, on pieces of paper, letters, wills, receipts... In an empty bath tub, water and my body find each other as a perfect mould and embrace; on the empty chair I sit and meditate or have supper...
Ha-ha... Aha... Such emptiness is more, and everywhere; determined.
In an empty quiet heart, Love finds its' way and enters it; tames it, rounds it up with much comfort, joy and warmth...
In that empty house one gets a flat available and moves in.
Oh, dear emptiness and stillness...find us, and enrich us with your existence, with silence and peace.

PERFECT POSTURE
Heather Cook

Those movements, clean and clipped,
would win her medals on the dance floor.
I hardly breathe as yards away
a roe deer high steps out from shadow
to stand erect and watchful on the lawn.
The fence is down, the barrier removed
between the wood and my suburban patch;
how soon the wild things come,
mocking my attempts to order an untidy world.

The roe deer visits daily, favouring the hour
when long grey afternoons give way to warmer light.
Her reddish coat gleams quietly.
she nuzzles fuchsias in their pots,
mouths plump rosebuds, plucks at seedlings,
freezes at a jackdaw's sudden swoop;
but then a yellow rambler dips, springs back,
a lush twig trailing and ignored.
I relish such disdain. I would buy her roses.

THE SPIDER AND THE CARELESS HUSBAND

Heather Cook

It’s not my job, cleaning out the plughole.
I found a spider swirled in chopped tomatoes
and raged against the guilty party:
the watchman who had failed to watch,
the thoughtless emptier of pans.

I laid my midget Martian on a snowy cloth,
watched his blobby body bleeding juice
into a seeping circle; I jumped to see
a current jerk his tangled legs
that braced in unison to raise him.

I was ridiculously pleased.
born aloft, sheltered by cupped hands,
my battered hero landed softly amongst ferns
and scuttled back to spiderdom.
I took a breath and made two cups of tea.

ON EARTH'S BREAST
Peter Corbett

The dark languid night passed slowly,
With the maritime shells of winter
Blowing from the west,
Breathing a heavy sign
Around the skeleton bones
Of the oak's broadway.
It's allee sweeping through
The secret territory of your imagination:
The childhood treasures exposed in old age,
Through the transient whispers of a summer's breeze
Or the fall of water onto lichen stones.

Look, those rooted mountains store history
In their layered heart,
Store the silence of the wild,
Remembered in a fleeting memory
Of some naked willow's dancing;
Where the yellow warbler's cry
Is heard over the autumn leaves,
And the honey-bee collects nectar
To feed the world and its distractions.

Now the oceans call to the sun's rise,
Another universe in miniature,
To reflect the blood-soaked clouds
And later the ghosts of falling rain;
They hide deep fissures
In love's longing,
Dissolving like light-snow
On earth's breast.
Then sleep comes from the shadows
Rearing the bliss, nameless, self-effulgent,
Each day a page of eternity
Blooming like a pregnant flower.

DRAGON'S TALES
Peter Corbett

This rooted space, earth-worn and ground down
With the autumn leaves of acer-blood,
Hijacked by the sprinkling of a blackbird's song;
With the dead mouths of crumpled flesh
Lying like a blanket
On the dawn's mannequin:
Love's warm caress decked
With lightning's words
Strewn over the hedgerows,
Tentacled shadows over stone walls
Moving like dragon's tails.

Now the sacred lichen grows
By the sun's fire:
For the bones of winter are near
Heralding the changes to nature's skin,
Like the threaded willow
Woven into pagan skeleton frames
In the fertile valley of yellow corn,
The wide track roving through deep woods;
Reborn again in Hermes's desire,
And lost in a world far away
Lost in the beating of waves
On some forgotten shore:

And in that moment
Merge and live in the Nut-sky forever.

WITH VOICES OF WILD LONGING

Peter Corbett

The tide-shadows beat the golden filaments of sand,
Dressed down the dunes of breasted turf,
And speak to the clean sunset
With voices of wild longing.

It is a desert now
Foregoing the islands of men;
Timeless, lying over the ebb and flow
Of centuries, the west wind
Bringing grey sheets of sullen clouds
Wassailing across an empty sky.

The Roman ash, dropping leaves like gold coins
On the seasoned earth,
With the solidarity catchers of dreams,
Watchful, alert, on the peninsula's bow:
A heavy globe of fading day,
As the striations of the years
Form banks of liquid stones
Just this side of the dissolving horizon.

Now the Great Mother sighs,
And her Origin bites deep
Into the Centre of things –
It forces open the winnower of wheat,
It seals the scar of birth.
It keeps the lotus flower alive.

THE SCARF

Philip Burton

There is a scarf longer than History. As with geological strata, each new era adds a section. The scarf is washed in water. Water is older than The Solar System.

Mesopotamian proto-alchemy
knew that the scarf flows, fills its function
as all things do, not as enemy
but as connection, a lifeline
back across the water which brought us here.

Greek and Egyptian alchemy –
applying Nature's chromaticity – shone
at sure-handed colourfast dyeing of drapery.
The scarf kept faith with:
the perch, the elephant-snout fish,
the water leopard,
                                        the barbel, and the bolti.
Artists pigmented the sphinx,
colour-washed the tombs of Beni Hasan,
yet no dyes, no toxins would bleed
into The Nile between Iken and Heracleion.

Now technology shreds the scarf
and cocktails it with sewage
along with nameless toxins known to persist
longer than The Pyramid of Khafre.

Then the vile muck is dried and baled
and sold to farms to be inhaled
by the precious soil, absorbed by corn and kale,
guileless gut, delicate entrail.

One day we'll retrieve
that ragged end of the sacrificed scarf
and, wrapping it round our cold industrial hearts,
make sane the garment industry.

THE INDIGO FIB
Philip Burton

Sandpaper, sandpaper, rub down the knee
of my new jeans to make it seem
I live my life mixing cement,
battling the sun, building my homestead
personally.

Sandpaper, sandpaper, scuff and erode
sfumato style, showing a guile
Leonardo da Vinci himself would applaud.

But what price Art: what price the guile
I'm so proud of the while?
Each distressed rip, gaping hole with frayed edge

tell only of wasted water, the toxic mess
the making of denim has caused to arise.

DISAPPOINTMENT
Helen Prescott

A tiny council flat of social housing repute
Behind a defunct red brick factory
Facing the rear misery-masonry
Cramped damp weary terraces
Pock-marked rickety stone side lane
Long forgotten in time
Grass sneaks through crevasses
Some distressed dog barks in a distant back-yard
Litter trod into pavements
An algae green slime fence
Snagged in a tree, a plastic bag waves surrender

The Street of Happy Sparrows
Plus the week's highlight trip to Morrison's for lunch
Friday's she checked-out the food bank
Before conversations with the local 'socialist'
About the state of the world
Which they were part of
Yet they would always be
Bent on disquietude
All they could not fix

One day the Poet Laureate arrived
To speak at the local Academy
She was not interested
Her desires were chatty cafes
Serving conglomerate coffee
And the day the revolution would come …
Alas it never did
Tomorrow was interminably the same as today
But all the sparrows were happy

NO MAN'S LAND
Helen Prescott

Three miles from the house and you enter 'No man's Land'. I take visitors there by car to show them how wild the land is only a short distance from so-called civilization. This is not 'No man's Land', only figuratively speaking. The locals know where it is but do they know what it is or even what went on up there? The place lends itself to mystery and adventure, romance, murder and even getting lost. Climbers, walkers, interlopers and elopers all made it here. Neither is it too remote unless you are well off the tracks. Gentle gradients and inviting hillsides of bracken, gorse and cotton grass can all be traversed as sheep look on from their stubbly pastures.

A fateful plane crash one wintry night made headline news. The flight came from the Isle of Man, never to return. Yet the incident was overshadowed by the Munich air disaster.

Friends of the king, opera singers and vandals plus the odd suffragette from Preston hell-bent on arson, all found their way up the slopes. A Scotsman died up there, others merely twisted their ankles tripping down precipitous slippery stone steps.

Once there was a grand view from the terrace and if you were lucky and the wind was blowing in the right direction you could hear the roar of a lion or bleat of a strange exotic creature.

Most of the pretty rhododendrons were grubbed up due to blight but the Japanese garden lake was opened up more with a sacred stone tortoise resting on the shore and mock-ancient Japanese shrines there to add peace and tranquility. Yet the bungalow with the ballroom ceiling decorated with the night's stars is long gone. This place has changed so much but what is it now but a leisure 'park' and moorlands hill where the snow lies in winter drifts.

Many views are blocked by over-grown trees, soon to be felled. Hiding in the woods had been the 'coiners' of old. The sounds now are of hiker's boots on the stone steps, bird song and distant livestock. Could it return to the wild outback it once was?

WATER
Helen Prescott

In 1923 a man called Christopher Long from Cambridge discovered the cave. He retraced the flow of water and there it was. A natural cave in the limestone hillside. As caves go it is big at four and a half miles long and is the largest show cave in Europe. Local miners blasted through the passage ways to make it more accessible. I joined a tour into the icy darkness. All was grey, white and black and for over an hour I felt like I had walked into a monochrome movie of the fifties.

There is much rain in this part of the North West and a few years ago the village was hit by a memorable flood but not as devastating as that at Hebden Bridge. Two rivers flow, the Twiss that becomes the Greta and the Doe which join up near the viaduct. They are quiet rivers tucked away from view as the village sits above looking down. I had not remembered the rivers from an earlier visit with the absence of gurgling, bubbling and splashing. Yet beneath my feet in that long cave where you must walk like a gorilla are torrents of gushing water, whilst the tumbling aqua can be very noisy as it crashes over boulders. Even in this drought the water is busy. Further inside the cave is an ancient deep lake but I didn't venture that far to witness this marvel.

No trains run anymore though two stations once existed, on either side of the viaduct where porters would take luggage to and fro. Two different railway companies owned the different lines and two stations were required. There were three lines in the area, the main one being Carlisle to Settle and Leeds.

The landscape is attractive with an abundance of dry stone walls penning in the sheep. Waterfalls are plentiful and an inspiring sight during the wet season. Often the small cafes are full of walkers, climbers, pot-holers, cave visitors and tourists all exploring the environment.

When I mentioned the viaduct, someone thought I was talking about Ribblehead. No there's one here but smaller and Settle has an even smaller one. A region of giant viaducts and Arnside across Morecambe Bay has one too. There is something creepy about these lofty arches looming overhead. Perhaps I feel unnerved due to its abandonment and state of disrepair and neglect. An empty feeling for one that was once loved but is now forgotten. The viaduct in the village is closed off and deemed a dangerous structure. It towers over the village as an immaculate conception of viaducts. A willful child could sneak a peep but it's firmly out of bounds, the village not wanting a reputation as a suicide centre.

People are familiar with caves, hillside walks and waterfalls, a pull for tourists but what of a landscape gardener and Sherlock Holmes? Is there a connection to this place? You bet there is. Thomas Mawson the eminent Victorian landscape gardener who created Rivington Gardens lived here as a child. His family came from the Garstang area. In 1870 his father built Prospect Cottage at Bank End which is unlike most cottages that skirt either side of the road in that the vista is back down the road and away from the village. The whole of the frontage comprises a series of wide glass windows though the property is a modest two up, two down with a steep drop on one side.

interesting sights until 1960 when the steam trains trundled across. In the front garden is a monkey puzzle tree, the only one in the village and a scattering of Scots pines.

During the days of steam travel, Sherlock was a common name in the area, as was Holmes. Arthur Conan Doyle married in the local church of St Oswald. His mother it transpired had lived in the area for thirty five years, so he knew the place well. His father had been an alcoholic and on developing mental illness was confined in an asylum in Edinburgh where he later died. Arthur never attended his father's funeral. His writing career had already begun and he didn't want the stigma of association with a so-called 'crazed' relative.

One day a newspaper proprietor called Sherlock from Liverpool was visiting the area when he was struck by lightning at the railway station and perished. Could he be the stimulus for the name Sherlock Holmes? A memorial window in the parish church is known as the 'Sherlock window'. However another suggestion is that the Holmes character was named after Oliver Wendell Holmes (1809-1894) American physician, writer, poet and father of the US Supreme Court of Justice.

The village makes nothing of these two connections – a landscape gardener and a crime and mystery novelist. The area must have influenced Conan Doyle.

At the end of his tales, Holmes disappears at a waterfall after a struggle with Moriarty but these are the famous Reichenbach falls of Switzerland rather than the torrents of North Yorkshire. On this hot June weekend, where am I?

GAIA'S FIRST FLIGHT

Bernadette Jordan

Gaia sits on her Nana's knee, just meters away from a deadly cold wind so strong it could rip flesh from bone. Her Nana, Jan reaches up to direct a cooling breeze on to her face.

Far away in the depths of Iceland's molten core, a great pressure is building. Magma is flowing along new fissures. Immense heat, molten rock.

Gaia points to the fragile ice crystals clinging daintily to the outside of the window. 'Angel dust' says Jan holding her grand-daughter firm in her arms, a guardian to this precious child. Together they admire the bulbous pink-tinted clouds in the distance, like Michelangelo's heavenly skies.

Far to the north, an Earth shifting power is building.

Gaia dozes off to the engine's heavy drone. She is riding the winds in a tube of still air. Jan senses the power that shifts them south over the countries of Europe. Immense forces 'mantra 'just trust, just trust...' she repeats to herself.

Scientists monitor Eyjaffallajokull, as it wakes from its slumber. Satellite images show the volcano inflating. Seisometers measure the vital signs of movement. Warnings are given. Evacuation imminent.

Flight 491 to Lanzarote hits a patch of turbulence. Monitors measure the forces. Warning signs flash. The plane bucks and dives, its wings flex. Jan wakes Gaia, lifts her into her own seat and straps her in.

An eruption sends a Seismic shock wave through Iceland's ash-strewn earth, as pressures alter, miles below the surface.

Gaia screams with sudden searing pain as her eardrum buckles to the changes in pressure. The wing tilts and the plane returns to an even keel. ''Here, suck on this,' says Jan. Gaia sucks hard and bites into a bright red sweet. Her ear feels better.

A crack appears on the flank of the volcano. Molten rock spews out, fiery and red. A line of searing heat stretches out for over a mile.

Jan screws up the sweet wrapper and twists it tight. Her mind is a whirlwind of pent-up emotion, excitement and fear, spin around each other.

The Earth shudders. Plumes of soot are released from the mouth of the exploding volcano. Silica forms into glass crystals, minute sharp

shards created from the contrast of hot and cold, shoot into the atmosphere.
The view through the window turns a blank white as the plane's engines suck in the cloud. Ice crystals turn in an instant to steam and the engines throw out gas and smoke. Burnt oil leaves streams of heat and dirty air, stretching out behind them for mile upon mile. Gaia snuggles into her blanket as the Earth's blanketing atmosphere is eroded.
Gasses are ejected, forming a pillar of smoke. The forces beneath continue to pump out ash.
Jan feels her heartbeat faster as the plane swings round and descends above the volcanic desert of Lanzarote. The plane passes through cloud. Gaia presses her nose to the window for her first view of palm trees and black sand, then she lurches forward with the reverse thrust of the engines.
Another explosion. Ash is thrust into the atmosphere 9 kilometres high.
Jan clutches her knees. The plane comes to a gentle landing. It is grounded.
Caught in the Jetstream, the ash from Iceland spreads and levels. Wind-herded fragments of silica, shrapnel-sharp make the skies unsafe for flight.
Jan listens to news of aircraft restrictions over the northern hemisphere. Bolts of lightning from inside the volcanic cloud are captured on film as the world wakes up to news of the eruption. Weather forecasters monitor wind speed and direction. Stranded passengers crowd the bars and beaches, wanting to be home. Screens show, a giant form being whipped by high altitude winds. It becomes like a writhing beast with limbs stretching across the sky. Its monstrous gaseous body could be sucked into an aeroplane's engines causing death and destruction. It lurks above them all like a vast Viking invasion of the skies.
And beyond the billowing brimstone cloud, the sun sets slowly, creating a spectacular scene. Immense cushiony clouds pillow a crescent moon in a sky that is clear of jet engine scribble. The upper atmosphere is silent for a one-week amnesty in the relentless assault of the aircraft.
Gradually glass fragments begin settling, becoming harmless displaced dust upon the earth. Meanwhile ten million stranded passengers make frantic plans to move.

Held high in the comfort of Jan's arms, Gaia boards the plane for home. The engines let out a fearsome roar. Oil displaced from beneath the ground is once more fired into the atmosphere.

And so, Gaia named after the earth goddess, came safely to land and humanity returned to normal. Soon the goddess Gaia may speak in a still small voice of calm that could be impossible to ignore.

WINDFARM

Ellena van Tebberen

I stand tall
A synchronized turbine,
As I levitate above the peat bog
In layered clouds,
My alien arms shimmer, intractable
On a scant horizon
I was once lost to the mists
In silk's enfold,
Remaining a ghostly rendition
To the wind torn hills,
Until shifting gusts
Tear apart the seeping haar,
Then the backdrop mountains
Rise in the distance.
My white stream-lined tower
Stands solid and implacable,
Midst sweeping hills
Where a cradled loch shivers.
As a wind turbine … do I add to
Or subtract from the landscape?
Not being a mathematician
I reserve my judgement.

MY LAWN
Tony Oswick

A mosaic of moss and meadow masquerading as a lawn,
drowned in depths of daisies, docks and dandelions,
wisps of green, green grass of home
in fairy rings of toadstools and not-so-magic mushrooms.

Though drowned in depths of daisies, docks and dandelions
it's my little haven of heaven,
with its fairy rings of toadstools and not-so-magic mushrooms,
untouched by raking, restoration or aeration.

It's my little haven of heaven.
But if I was a sower - or Percy Thrower with a mower -
I'd do raking, restoration and aeration
and repair those threadbare patches.

But I'm no sower - or Percy Thrower with a mower.
My mosaic of moss and meadow masquerading as a lawn
and all those threadbare patches
is my green, green grass of home.

ROOTED IN FRIENDSHIP

Tony Oswick

I watered you this evening. The watering can's heavy these days and it's such a long way down the garden for someone my age. But I had to do it. Just one more time.

Grandpa was proud of you. "I planted him in 1921, Norman," he always liked to tell me. "Look after him and he'll always look after you." And, since then, our family's looked after you while you've watched over our house, like a king surveying his subjects. Grandpa originally intended planting a tree for every son and daughter he had - good job father was an only child or the garden would've resembled a jungle. Mind you, with all the weeds and brambles, it looks like a jungle now.

Do you remember when I used to climb up and collect your apples inside my shirt? Mother told me to be careful but I never fell off, I knew you'd always protect me. She made such wonderful pies with those apples. Sometimes, I'd climb you just for fun, take a book with me and hide among your leaves. And I don't think you'll ever forget the time I scratched Evelyn Carrington's initials on your trunk. I was only seventeen. She was my only love but she found someone else. Of course.

Two years ago I noticed something wrong. We'd just celebrated your hundredth birthday but, that summer, your blossom wasn't so attractive, your leaves not so fleshy, your apples not so plentiful. 'Monty Don's Every Day Gardening' said that apple trees, especially old ones like you, needed plenty of water.

I thought a can of water every evening might do the trick. It didn't though, did it? Last year, you had just a scattering of leaves and no blossom or fruit at all. The birds who usually secreted themselves in your branches and leaves must have felt so exposed. I carried on watering every evening, a can-full around your roots, and prayed it would work, act like a magic potion. But life's not like that, is it? Your bark began to peel like a scab from a sore, your trunk turned wrinkly and I felt as sad as you looked.

I got a man around but you didn't like him, did you? He poked your trunk, broke off a branch and shook his head. "Honey fungus," he declared. Said apple trees like you usually only lived for seventy years. Said you'd done well to survive over a hundred.

The trouble is, you've *always* been there. You *belong*. But is it fair to leave you looking like a skeleton? If only I'd started watering you earlier, perhaps I could've saved you?

The man's coming tomorrow at ten. Said it'll take three hours. All that will be left is a twelve-inch stump. I don't want to be there but I will. We'll both have to be brave. But the garden will look so strange without you.

You do understand, don't you?

PIGEON POST

Dorothy Snelson

She sipped her tea as she looked through the kitchen window, admiring her garden. It was a windy day and the trees were swaying and the flowers dancing in the stiff breeze. Suddenly a pigeon landed on the fence with a leaf bizarrely wrapped around its head, blown there by the wind. It was such a comical scene that she laughed aloud. As she turned away, she thought angrily, that pigeons and leaves had become a major issue for her lately.

It hadn't always been that way. For years, she and Mr Jenkins had lived next door to each other, widow and widower, in perfect harmony. Both of them lovers of gardening, wild life, birds, bees and trees and shrubs. Until, that is, Mr. Jenkins had suffered a sudden stroke and died. A couple in their fifties with two teenage children bought the house. The wife was very pleasant, and the kids were quiet and hardly ever seen. The husband was the problem. He was soon complaining about everything to do with the garden.

'Those trees need pruning. They're too tall. I'm getting all the leaves in my garden. I'm forever having to sweep up' he said. The next day it was

'I don't know why you have to have a bird table. All these birds you're attracting. There's bird dirt everywhere. All over my shed and the kitchen window. We'll be having rats before long. All that seed falling on the ground. We'll be overrun.'

It was wearing her down. A few weeks later an old friend who had started a bit of a gardening business when he retired, came to cut her conifer hedge. She called him in for a cup of tea and slice of cake.

'Your fruit cake would win prizes, Jane' he said, as he sat in the kitchen chatting. Then he changed tack and said

'How do you find this new chap next door? He came out whilst I was working on the hedge and said'

'Are you cutting that apple tree down a bit and there's several others need pruning. They're getting to be a damned nuisance. Leaves everywhere.'

'I told him I was only doing what you had told me to do. Anything else he'd have to take up with you. He grunted then and went back inside.'

She told Bill about the problems she'd been having since the new family moved in.

'I avoid going out in my garden when he's out' she said. 'It's such a pity, as I love pottering as you know. I feel it will just invite another conversation about my trees and the birds and how I need to do something about them.'

'What do you say to him when you do see him?' Bill asked.

'I just mutter something about waiting until my son comes.'

'But Martin's in Canada' Bill said.

'Well he doesn't know that…yet' she said, with a shrug. 'I know it's just delaying the day when I have to confront the problem properly, but I suppose when I do, I'll have to see if we are both prepared to compromise. I don't want to live with bad feeling. I've been happy here. I'm just hoping I can be happy again.'

When Bill had left, she started to worry again about the situation next door but despite her best efforts, she struggled to come up with a solution, that wouldn't mean sacrificing many of the things that she loved about her garden. Trees chopped down, birds banished and instead of a pleasing landscape, something bland and boring.

A week later, she received a phone call from Bill, the gardener.

'Do you get the local Gazette, Jane?' he said. To which she replied

'I do, but I haven't read the latest yet. Been busy with stuff for church.

'Take a look at that latest one' he said mysteriously. 'I think you'll find something to interest you' and left it at that.

Intrigued she fished the paper out of the magazine rack. On the fourth page was a photograph she recognised instantly. It was her neighbour, suited and booted, and standing with his Jasmine, his daughter, the mayor and several other people, in a formal pose. Jasmine was holding some sort of award and smiling brightly. The headline said 'ECO-WARRIOR JASMINE WINS AWARD.' The article went on to describe how Jasmine, aged fifteen, had championed several projects at school and in her guide troupe. These had involved introducing wildlife corridors, planting trees, and providing nesting boxes for birds, and wildlife habitats for birds and bees. Her smiling father had been an encouraging influence, and was right behind her in her efforts to get people living at one with nature.

'Well. Fancy that 'she said with a grin. Be a bit difficult for him to quibble about the birds and trees in my garden now, when I drop a hint that I've seen this article. Maybe I'll just tell him to congratulate Jasmine, when next I see him?'

The sun had started to come out. Perhaps she would have a potter in the garden this afternoon she thought. If she saw 'Eco Warrior Senior' whilst out there, they could have a chat about nest boxes and planting trees. After all, he was practically an expert in the field, according to the Gazette. She chuckled to herself.

'Get out of that one if you can.'

IF YOU GO DOWN IN THE WOODS TODAY
Dorothy Snelson

'It was eight months ago' Louise said softly. 'There will never be a right time to move on, but perhaps this is a chance to do something that matters.'
She closed her eyes and looked back on the years of caring for her husband who had dementia, failing sight and hearing loss. The end came suddenly. A chest infection that turned to pneumonia and within two weeks he died, leaving her bereft.
She had tried to pick up the pieces of her former life but socialising alone had been strange and she still hadn't adjusted to her new status.
She glanced at the newspaper article and the contact details. Before she could change her mind she opened her laptop and fired off an e mail and then sat back wondering if anything would come of it.
It wasn't long before she found out. Woodland Trust were inviting her to a meeting of new volunteers at their headquarters in a local manor house owned by English Heritage. The vast estate, that had belonged to the owners of the Hall, had been sold to Woodland Trust. It was mainly moorland and in the past had been a hive of activity. There were farms, mines, a brick works and ale houses catering for the workers. Little shanty towns grew up and pedlars traversed the moors selling their wares. All this, except for the tenanted farms, had gone and nowadays the moors were a haven for wildlife and walkers. Woodland Trust, as custodians of the land, had ambitious plans and ideas to improve access for local people and promote interest in what they were doing. Louise felt a thrill of excitement and stirring of interest in what the ranger was relating. It would be good to get involved in something so big and worthwhile, even if she would be a small cog in the wheel. She felt sure that she would benefit too. The fresh air and exercise would be good for her physical wellbeing and the social aspects would improve her mental health. It was a win, win situation and she volunteered willingly.
At first she was assigned to litter picking, a mundane yet necessary activity. Surprisingly she found that she quite enjoyed it. There was a sense of achievement in tidying hedgerows and paths and thinking that you might be saving wildlife from the harm plastics or glass could cause. She could chat with passers-by and other members who might be about the same task. She made friends and often would have a coffee with hem later at the café in the Hall.

Later she progressed to balsam bashing, when the volunteers tried to eradicate this invasive species which threatened to prevent native plants from growing. It meant wellies and gloves, as it was prevalent in ditches and on the banks of streams but could be pulled up by hand easily. They worked in a group, in Spring which was the best time to tackle it and there was a sense of camaraderie and sometimes they even sang together. She loved those days, especially when it was fine and dry and they took a packed lunches and sat around chatting and laughing. It was good to feel a part of something so worthwhile, and to be contributing, even in a small way to helping nature thrive.

One day whilst having coffee with Matt, the ranger, he asked if she was interested in doing more training. She could train to take guided walks and also to speak to organisations about the work of the Woodland Trust. She jumped at the chance.

Her grandchildren were always eager to hear about her activities and once her training was complete, and she felt confident, she offered to give a little talk to Joshua's Forest School. Soon she was being invited to Emily's school to watch Emily deliver a little talk to her classmates about nature and her Gran's work at Woodland Trust. She felt proud to sit with the parents and grandparents and listen to Emily talking about all the good work the volunteers, like her own gran, did.

The local Dementia Carers often used rooms at the Hall for activities, or the café for meet ups. A guided walk for carers and cared for was scheduled to take place the following week and Matt, mindful of Louise's role as a carer in the past, asked if she would like to take the walk.

'I hope it is not too soon or something that might upset you 'he said. 'I just thought that you would be the ideal person to lead them.'

She didn't need to think twice.

'I would love to Matt' she said.

She had the most magical morning leading the group and progressing at the rate of the slowest couple. She helped push wheelchairs, chatted with the carers and felt a real empathy with them. She pointed out flora and fauna and recently planted trees and surprise herself with the knowledge she had built up over the previous six months.

'Was it really only six months ago that it started' she said to herself at the end. 'So much learned, so many friendships made, so much pride in what I am doing to help the environment' she thought.

She would be forever grateful to the advert that started it all.

Hedgerow by Inches

Shauna Corrigan

Hawthorn
Spring has shaken a
Dream of blushing lace along
The tender branches –

Where

Thimbleberry
Scraps of sunlight snagged
On cursive brambles flicker
In golden hyphens –

And

Cobweb
Slide in lithe, haunting
Notes along mellifluous
Strings with easy grace –

As,

Linnet
Nocked arrow poised, her
Tail a bright slice of agile
Silver sleek with wind –

She spies

Blackberries
Sharpening flashes
Of wry piquancy glossed
In savage colour –

And then, too,

Elderberries
Clustered opulence
Of occult jet in neat orbs
Gilding livid stems –

While

Hedge Mustard
In the breeze, summer's

Light flutters gold in shards caught,
Gleaming, in green nets –

And, in competing colours,

<u>Common Dog Violet</u>
Empresses with shy
Eyes bow to each other, robed
In scalding purple –

Until, inevitably,

<u>Crab Apple</u>
Autumn's crisp breath has
Fired each round red bead to a
Fine glassy finish –

Before,

<u>Dormouse</u>
Shuffling twilit snow
With lightening paws; blink- a flash
Of fleeting whiskers-

And suddenly, all that remains is

<u>Barberry Carpet Moth</u>
Soundless in supple
Damask; soft, subtle smudge on
This slant of moonlight –

That plays tricks,
Conjuring the past
From blank, bare, branchless ground.

THE TRIAL
Sue Gerrard

The pristine white court seemed timeless far beyond the depth and understanding of Hugh's experience. He had no idea how he had ended up here in the coffin like dock, on trial facing masked jurors. His taut skin bristled and was overstretched around his plump frame, every hair on his head hurt and his eyes were growing out of their sockets.

The judge was an anonymous, huddled heap hidden behind a grey tumbling wig, black mask and swaddled in blood red robes. The thud of his mallet brought Hugh back to reality; the jury was returning. He looked for comfort to his lawyer who had been foisted upon him, but the non-receptive eyes told him everything.

The jurors' weary feet slowly trudged in, scraping the white tiled floor, like members of a chain gang. They were defeated by worldly cares which had been thrown upon them.

'Have you reached a verdict?' the judge's gravel voice asked: 'How do you find the defendant, guilty or not guilty?'

The chief juror, his grainy voice came through a golden mask as he said: 'Guilty on all counts.'

Hugh swayed. What had he done other than try to live a good life? He worked hard, paid his taxes, looked after his wife, indulged his children, and walked the dog.

'Mr Hugh Mann, you have been found guilty on all counts but before I pass sentence each juror will talk about your crimes.'

'What crimes?' he asked bewildered.

The golden masked juror said: 'You willingly visited my unspoilt beaches, walked on age- old sand and contaminated it with rubbish causing my decline.'

A second said from behind the sky-blue mask: 'You condemned me, changed me from joyous, bright blue with free spirited birds for company to a black sky turning pure heavens into shade. You made me the carrier of smog and illness. Birds and now other creatures lie dead in my Mother's garden.'

'I don't know your Mother. 'Hugh said.

Another juror spoke from behind the navy-blue mask: 'My clean waters once flowed freely caressing shores, running over ancient river stones. Here fish and sea creatures settled, coral grew, and underwater plants flourished. Now these are destroyed. It is a plastic graveyard and underwater rubbish garden. My arteries are full of your waste, my heartbeat fading.'

Hugh put his head in his hands, all he had tried to do was live a good life.

The sunshine yellow masked figure said: 'You drove your car instead of walking, used barbecues to eat and caused my glowing face to be covered with a grimy black mask. Now I cannot shine as I should, illuminate the horizons as I want to do. You have brought darkness where once there was only light. My Mother told me that you were my friend.'

The pace of accusations intensified, and bitter words came from behind a silver masked female juror: 'My Mother told me that you would let me shine. I was born to shine, bright pin pricks of light in a dark night sky, beautiful to see but your need for constant light, artificial day, my stars. I cannot be seen; I lie forgotten in an ever-contaminated world.'

'I don't know your Mother.' Hugh wearily said again.

'Everyone knows Mother Earth.' the deep voice stated from behind his brown earth mask: 'You took my soil age-old, generous, loved and poisoned it so that nothing would grow then filled me full of chemicals to force me to yield that which I once gave freely. I am poisoned, I am corrupted, I am dying. You have killed my Mother and you are killing me.'

Hugh was beginning to understand but it was too late. He had only tried to live a good life.

A small voice said from behind a russet mask: 'I once brought fruit, my brothers leaves, my sisters flowers. We were the trees that covered the earth absorbed the harmful poisons allowing you to breathe. Now we are bare, barren limbs twisted in agony fit only for the funeral pyre.'

Hugh was descending into guilt. He had not known or understood what he was doing. If I could reset time I would he thought but now a voice from behind a chalk white mask said: 'I am the rock of ages. I have guarded the coastline, supported your houses, sheltered birds, been home to warning beacons, welcomed you home, seen you safely away but never have I faced an enemy like you.'

'Now we are crumbling, falling on the sands, crashing into seas and are condemned to oblivion.'

There they stood the twelve jurors and Hugh had nothing he could say to them. It was too late.

The judge then spoke, after putting on his black cap: 'Hugh Mann you have been found guilty of poisoning and suffocating Mother Earth and her children, have you anything to say?'

Hugh stuttered in a muffled voice: 'I only wanted to live a good life.'

'It is this selfish attitude coupled with the mindless pursuit of pleasure which has brought you here and us to the brink of destruction. I will now pass sentence.'

Hugh quivered. So, it was death.

The judge spoke: 'I am going to send you back to where you came from, to live with what you have created on Mother Earth and so you can right the wrongs you have done.'

OVERCOMING FOMO

Jennifer Palmer

'I'm moving to the countryside,' Julia announced one day to her London friends.

'But you love city life,' her friends said. 'What on earth will you do all day long without the theatre or cinema or wine bars to distract you, for God's sake?'

'Fear of missing out won't be a concern,' she said. 'It's not as if I'll be cut off from the world. I'll have email and the internet, TV and Netflix. By the way, you're all welcome to visit any time you like.'

A couple of months later, Julia had packed up and gone. The house she moved into was one of two cottages, originally connected to a farmstead. There was a barn nearby that had recently been converted into a dwelling, but otherwise things were much the same as they'd always been.

'How are you finding life in the outback?' a friend asked sarcastically when they were talking on the phone.

'It's great,' Julia said. 'We've been having the hedges cut back. They'd shot up so much that you couldn't see over them. Farmers don't have time for hedge laying any more. They employ local contractors to cut them back, but it leaves loads of spikes on the road, much to the aggravation of the postman, who is forever getting punctures. The gaps in the walls don't get repaired either due to a lack of drystone wallers. When you think about how long they've been there, it's amazing the walls are still standing. It's the rain and frost that does for them.'

It was a while before she heard from that friend again.

'They don't know what they're missing,' Julias comforted herself with. 'They are still breathing in all that polluted air along the Marylebone Road. No amount of green policies will get rid of that, whereas here it's clean, fresh air all day long.'

On fine days she went out for walks. Sometimes she'd go uphill and have the downward part to look forward to. Sometimes she'd go downhill first. According to Michael Mosley's on the radio, up and down were both good. Uphill was good for the heart and lungs, whereas downhill strengthened the leg muscles.

'Why don't you come and visit,' she suggested again to friends. 'If you come in the springtime there will be bluebells, primroses, water

Aven and marsh marigolds. Or come in May when the hawthorn hedges will be white with blossom. They look like a Van Gogh painting. In summer there are red campions and meadowsweet in the hedgerows. Last year I came upon some Canterbury Bells, which always appear at the same time of year and in the same stretch of bank. There are purple vetches, gooseberries, and later on blackberries and sloes, to make jam and sloe gin.'

But no one seemed keen. She recalled how living in London was like living in a bubble. When you lived there, it took a gigantic effort to summon up the energy just to go on a day trip, let alone on a weekend one. It was as if the rest of the country didn't exist. Eventually she abandoned trying to persuade them and stuck to email offerings.

'The wild roses are long gone. Soon there will be rosehips. In the fifties people picked them for charity because of the Vitamin C they contained. They were sent away in bulk to be made into rosehip syrup. It was a habit that continued long after the war.'

'The only tree you see on the moor is the hardy hawthorn, bent double by the prevailing wind. There are buzzards and kestrels up there and sky larks singing and dive bombing to the ground. You hear curlews, calling across the valley. Last year there were three pairs of lapwings nesting in the bull rushes. I don't know how many of their young survived. There are so many crows and magpies hovering around these days.'

'There aren't many of the old established farming families left. Most of us are *newcomeduns.* There are people here from all walks of life. It's like anywhere. Some people prefer to keep to themselves. Others like to mix. It's good to rub up against people with different opinions. It forces you to challenge your ideas. The people I meet on walks are into wildlife. We compare notes on flower and bird species.'

'Of course, there are drawbacks, like when it snows, and the roads get iced up and you can't get out or when a gale blows down the high voltage wires and causes a power cut. But you soon get used to that.'

SWANS
Sam Szanto

We watch two swans perform a synchronised
courtship, facing each other, ruffling their feathers,

lifting their wings and bowing their heads
together, forming the shape of a heart.

I tell my daughter they mate for life,
she giggles at the thought of *romance*,

I don't tell her it's probably about survival,
but say they have amazing memories

and don't forget acts of kindness or meanness.
No, love, let's not test that out.

As she laughs at one's nasal trumpeting,
I take her hand to lead to the playground.

FOURTEENTH

Kirsty Softly

No clouds
In my sky
I don't know why.

Is it scandalous neglect?
Zero control?

I can't imagine winter, or the perfect Sunday
And spring feels miles away
to my out-stretched, begging hands.

What happens when we reach:
Hostile
Inclusive
Collapse?

THE WORLD ROUND AND GIVING

Sue Gerrard

The world round and giving was shaken,
taken piece by piece by those living.

A field here was stripped of sheep,
cleared of crops, as factories raised
their smoking heads instead.

A river there was taken,
Fish daily swam away; water
dark with waste, terminally unclean
as coal ships and steam boats
left behind their poisons.

A gentle hill here was sliced in two
making fragile flowers homeless.
Instead, venomous silver snake roads
lie where butter cups once grew.
They carry leaden loads across the hills,
black trail leading to the mills.

A lush green wood was flattened here
Leaving birds and animals without a home.
In place of woodland splendour
are concrete houses and industrial hives
which sting the air with smoke.

The world round and giving was shaken
And should now be restored by the living.

ADAM'S WORLD
Bernadette Jordan

Adam admires a picture on the wall, undulating hills, green against blue, beautifully framed.
Behind the glass he sees a stilled horizon, a captured scene, edited to perfection.
Here is colour without movement, Summer without scent.
Silent contentment reaches him, without the bite of reality.
He's trapped between picture frame and window frame with
Glassy safety and a single scene.

And so, Adam escapes to nearby hills,
Walks away until his gaze reaches an unbroken horizon beyond a faraway shore.
Distance draws lines of greyness, land gives way to the sheen of sea.
He crouches down low beneath the cover of a mottled clump of heather.
A breeze plays with the light, grass-waves spread,
Cloud shadows are scudding across the hillside, multiplying colours into myriad hues.
A skylark's frantic love song draws his gaze into unattainable heights.
This little bird is shifting swiftly through shafts of light, ascending into invisibility.
Adam loses his airy focus and settles his gaze back to the ground, easing his neck.

Returning home windswept, chilled, invigorated, Adam settles to download photographs.
His computer is an alchemy of earth and human ingenuity, lithium, oil and sand.
He distils the scenes he's seen, sees again the views of sky and grass and coast.
Like a timelord he has the power to stop in one moment, to still a slice of time and space, to preserve the light,
To keep, enhance or share.
He looks again at detail he missed, the shine of sun through the skylark's wing revealing the intricacy of a feather.

Remembered intimacy.

Yet possession is not Adam's gift.
Memory eludes,
time distorts,
the screen saves an illusion.

Escaping afresh he walks again into replenished reality.
Each day, each hour, each minute and second and blink of the eye;
each encounter is his,
A 'Now' that is unique.
Walking wakens life, unstoppable, unrepeatable, true.

… And yet even this is not enough.
Adam still has the urge to show and share.
…And where in his world is Eve?
Perhaps she is trapped in another picture, but that's another story.

UNPLUGGED

Isabel Harry

I became a vegan on the day my father died. When my first child was stillborn, I joined an environmental activist group. When my husband left me, I decided it was time to renew my connection with nature. It seemed the only thing to do.

The day Richard fled from my life, I bought an off-the-grid cabin in the woods. My fourteen-year-old son had been withdrawn and forlorn since his father left, and I wondered if a week spent in the wilderness together might put his heartache into perspective, as nature so often did for me. Maybe attending to the environment would give him the peace of mind to finally move forward.

We said little on the drive to the cabin. Toby spent most of the journey with his head slouched over his phone, much to my dismay. I turned my attention from him and let the mazework of forest and wildlife consume me as it raced past the window.

"Leave your phone in the car," I reminded him once we arrived. He mumbled something in response, but I let its meaning brush past me.

The wooden cabin was a beacon of peace amid the twining branches of the surrounding trees. Dappled shade rendered the cabin into a picture out of a story book. I knew my boy and I would find solace here.

I spoke into the stiff silence between us, pointing out the water pump and the bench to the right-hand side of the house. Inside, I showed him the fireplace and the densely stocked food cupboards. When I'd finished, he asked, "What am I meant to do here?"

I threw my arms wide to the forest around us. "Take in the environment. There's so much more to the world than just your phone."

"I know that!" The defensiveness in his tone surprised me. "I don't need a week in an off-the-grid cabin to prove that I love nature!" He seemed about to say more, then snapped his lips shut and stalked off into the forest.

I pumped a bucket full of water to distract myself. He was hurting. Perhaps if he could draw himself from his pain and immerse himself in the natural world, he would be okay. I would do everything in my power to help him.

That night, we sat in separate armchairs by the fire, an empty couch between us. His face was fixed in brooding contemplation as he stared into the fire. I added my voice to the crackling flames. "I think it will feel good to live without electricity and running water for a few days. Humans have gotten so used to these luxuries that we forget to appreciate them. We forget the toll our actions take on the environment, and so we don't conserve resources."

"Please, mum," Toby spoke wearily. "Can you just give it a rest?"

He wasn't ready to let my words console him yet. He wasn't ready to find refuge in the knowledge that the world had bigger problems than us. That night, I kept that measly comfort for myself.

#

We spent the following days walking, eating, and contemplating. My time with Toby was peppered with small talk and pleasantries, but mostly, we remained in silence. A few times I tried to spark meaningful conversation between us, to no avail. He barred himself from my attempts, and sometimes, I thought he was even disdainful of them.

As afternoon trundled into dusk on our fourth day, I snapped.

"Toby, why don't you just try? You've spent the past few days in such a beautiful location, and all you've done is sulk! If you just took a little pride in the world around you… it would help you get through this difficult time. I love the environment—"

"You don't love the environment!" The words erupted from Toby like lava from a long dormant volcano. It was all I could do not to stagger back in shock. "This whole trip has nothing to do with the environment! It's all about *you.* You can't stand that dad left us, so you make us hide out in the woods like cowards. You don't even ask me what I want!"

I could hardly form words around the lump in my throat. Was he right? I had told myself we were coming to this cabin for Toby. Losing myself in my love for nature had always been my refuge in dark times, and I wanted to give that to him. All this time, have I just been hiding? Was retreating to my obsession with the environment only a means of making myself feel better?

"I'm… so sorry." Tears accosted me, and I couldn't say more without breaking down. Mercifully, Toby walked away, giving me the time that I needed.

It was something Richard would have done.

#

That evening, we talked for the first time in years. Not about nature or saving water, but about things that had too long remained unsaid. We drove home first thing the following morning. As the car rumbled onto the motorway, I resolved to start caring for the environment selflessly. I would not hide in nature anymore, but love it how it was meant to be loved. Just as I loved my son.

ENVIROMENTAL PLIGHT
Aldis Kreicbergs

A soft gentle breeze on a hot summer's day
Rustling leaves and grass, wafting blues away.
The wind changes, gentleness turns to rage
Causing destruction, going on a rampage
Provoking stormy seas, tossing ships around
Felling trees, reducing houses into rubble on the ground
Stoking raging forest fires, gales fanning the deathly flame
But without erratic winds, earth would not be the same.
Nature is beautiful but can be so cruel.
Using the planet's resources as her fuel
Mankind is like nature
Unpredictable
Kind, evil, cruel
Indictable
"Lessons have been learned"
Is a common phrase
Bandied around by politicians
Whilst looking sideways
"We learn from our mistakes"
Is what they always say
But carry on making them
Day after day
Power-crazy leaders cause the most harm
Their lies and propaganda cause alarm
For death and destruction they are to blame
But they do not care they have no shame
We are killing each other, tearing our planet apart
Destroying wildlife, breaking Mother Nature's heart
Polluting the air and poisoning the seas
Fouling rivers and destroying trees
God created Man in his own image.
So the Bible says
Perhaps we'll understand why
One of these days
Was human creation a huge mistake
Giving Mother Nature a big headache

LIFE AFTER DEATH

Aldis Kreicbergs

The ravages of a hate-filled war linger all around
Blood and decaying corpses swathing the ground
Only the wind stirs in this gruesome barren place
Mother Nature again scarred by the human race
Then nourishing rain falls and mingles with blood
Feeding a solitary seed submerged in black mud
A tiny green shoot warily imbibes the fresh air
Sensing the stench of war is no longer there
White petals spread out as the daisy grows
More shoots appear and bathe in the sun
After the pointless killing has nature won
The battlefield of death springs into life
Beauty and harmony replacing strife

IT TAKES TIME
Bernadette Jordan

Germination happened in a split second three hundred and fifty-six years, four months and twenty-one days ago. The acorn was buried by a squirrel that died a very long time ago.
Age did not weary this tree. Year after year new rings of growth increased its girth. Each spring more and more leaves unfurled. Twigs turned to branches, zig zagging towards the light. Each summer it fed a multitude of insects. Children played beneath its boughs and lovers met within its shade. Each Autumn it scattered the ground with leaves. The ancestors of that squirrel who buried the acorn found plenty of nuts of their own. Winter looked like death, but this tree was a harbour for life. A jay nestled in the shelter of a hollow, ladybirds tucked themselves tight into folds of bark, and slug eggs lay in clusters close to its roots.
Cotton, coal and clogs stamped their mark across the land. A town engulfed the woodland, but this oak had its place in the crook of a stream. It withstood the siege like a castle with a moat. Every town must have its park and this tree became 'The Playground Tree.' But land is scarce on this overcrowded island and there is no real calculation for the value of a tree.
When trees die naturally, they decline over decades, feeding others in their wake. This mighty oak was dead within an hour. Watch it happen.

The chainsaw team arrive with trailer, truck and chipping machine.
Ropes are rigged, harnesses clipped, and the saw begins to scream.
Smoke and sawdust mingle. Huge branches crash to the ground gouging up turf.
Soon the oak is shorn.
A thirty second pause and the attack begins again.
A gaping wedge is cut deep into the trunk then the saw is repositioned at the other side.
Tree rings marking each year's growth are sliced in a split second.
With a groan from deep within its core the tree comes thundering down.
This living being is no more than a heap of timber.
An hour is all it takes. The tree has gone forever.

The town closed in on the island that was once a park, like the closing of a great green eye. Life shut down. Ladybirds were pulped with the tree and slugs were buried under concrete, only the jay flew free. He took with him an acorn in his beak. He flew above the shops and warehouses, factories and streets. He flew to the hills and rested. Instinct had drawn him to a quiet place. He worked a patch of turf with his beak, plucking and flicking the grass to one side. That jay planted the acorn well. Now all it needs is a little space and lots and lots of time. With many centuries ahead the oak may yet have a second chance.

SLIOCH

Rose Martin

Standing atop a sandstone castle,
Above a loch’s archipelago;
Where to set foot is to step back
To the ancient wildwood untouched.

Below sheer slopes a craggy moor unfolds,
Streams pattern a wilderness untrod;
A summer wind blows from the horizon’s sea
Brushing my face with wandering caress.

Beckoned by the sublime perspective,
On the highest peak my gaze catches;
A golden eagle soaring
Below me on outstretched wings.

BRAERIARCH

Rose Norman

To see the heart of true wilderness unfold,
Seek granite uplands, vast to behold;
The space above and the space below –
Ice age sculptures from glacial flow.
In a bleak wild swept by frequent storms
Stands a lonely sentinel of the Cairngorms.

A plateau spreads westwards wide,
Nowhere from winter winds to hide;
Subarctic flora hugs the ground,
No barrier to the wind is found.
All of nature's elements expose
A realm where no visitor can impose.

The stark and glorious land casts its spell –
The weight of trivialities dispel.
Alas the need to retreat;
For no man can sit upon this seat.
Evermore to reminisce with awe
A place of magic and ravens' caw.

BROKEN SPECTRE
Rose Norman

Enter another world of mountain mists -
There's chance that gathered cloud in sunlight
Should hide on peak ascent or ridge's sweep
The subtle gleam of colour plain in sight.

An immense shadow leaps across the hill
Unites a secret mist-enabled tryst –
Your figure circled bright in rainbow glow;
Our worlds collide – we pause to bridge their midst.

A transient beauty haunts the space between
Returns my gestures, reaching arms out wide,
And stepping where I step across the haze;
Sibling of dark and light so magnified.

Should fog then wane or mass - impeding sun
That apparition wavers - fades – dispels.
Forget-me-not until we meet again,
Memories long endure without farewells.

STOMPING GROUND

Kaye Outhwaite

Getting ready for the afternoon patrols, Willow devoured her food. It tasted bitter now, matching the sour metallic scent in the air. The stench of machinery had been around for the past two years. It contaminated everything.

It was mid-afternoon, which meant the motor engines would be firing up soon. The apprehension had driven many of the elders in the warren to jittering bundles of fur. Their fear rooted them to the spot. The kits in the warren sought their mother's protection. The frenzied sprints of young ones always led to scenes of unjust vengeance. The remaining adults had long ago been consumed by madness. They bit and nipped at the kits' toes to prevent them from reaching their mothers.

Willow grimaced at the all-too-familiar sight. What had become of them? They used to care for each other, but now hate was all that proliferated. Shaking her head she crawled through the central tunnel and out of the top bolt hole.

When Willow surfaced, the foul odour intensified, making her nose curl. Looking about her, the rest of the patrol appeared from the remaining bolt holes. Willow was never prepared for the devastation above ground. Each time it made her stomach quake.

As Willow scanned the landscape, she remembered how the warren would lay under the sunlight whilst nibbling refreshing cool grass. This was all gone, replaced with a thick sickly sludge of mud and decay. At the top of each hill there used to be trees providing shelter for patrols. These had been the first things severed from the land. Willow wished the warren had known what this signalled two years ago. They could have tried to emigrate to another field, tried to find salvation. Now it was too late, the warren deprived of nutrients for months.

Many were too weak to make the journey.

The hills themselves sat at the edge of the field, hugging the terrain with a mother's embrace. The warren itself was built into the side of one of these. The kits would play games together on the hills, daring each other to reach the very top. Willow remembered the cheeky

laughter from the kits as mothers chastised their children. If only that was all they had to worry about now. This was all gone. The hillsides were replaced with hunks of grey, and there was a slab of it encroaching on the warren.
Every day the grey expanded. This was always preceded by the heavy hands. They always brought devastation to everything in their vicinity. Looking around her, Willow could see these gluttonous machines advancing. Their deafening roar reverberated around Willow's chest. Inside of each hand was a man. Both seemed to move together with ease. It was difficult to tell where the machine began and the man ended.
Spluttering along, the heavy hands left behind a sweaty trail of engine oil. They churned up the earth as they tore straight for the warren. Willow stomped her feet as hard as she could to warn those below. The heavy hands continued to advance. Desperately, Willow carried on stomping, her feet slapping against the water-logged earth. Her fellow patrol members must have seen the danger now too, as they joined in. Agonisingly the patrol pounded the earth.
They all hoped someone in the warren below would hear them and escape.

The heavy hands' engines snarled at Willow, their pace speeding up as the clanking tracks landed upon the grey slab. The heavy hands reached the warren and extended their arms towards the heavens. Suddenly there was silence. It felt like many minutes passed. Willow looked up, the sunlight blinding her view. Fear gripped her now. All she could do was stare at the cold arm of death.
Without warning, the arm of a hand came hurtling down, splattering a patrol member into pieces. The nails of the hand scrapped through the mud and what remained of the rabbit. The hand transported the sludge into the air and twisted its arm sideways. Willow held her breath as the hand abruptly tilted and poured its tumorous waste on top of her.
Willow's ears rang. All she could think of was stomping her feet to warn the others. She flexed her rear muscles, preparing to emit a loud thump, but she couldn't move. The earth thrown on top of her was holding her feet firm. A loud pounding noise above her told her more soil was being thrown on top of her. The acidic pollution from the contaminated soil made her eyes water. It was getting harder to breathe.

The artificial war-cry of the heavy hands was becoming muffled. It was being replaced by a new, organic sound. The sound thudded. Its waxing and waning reminded Willow of being a young kit drinking milk from her mother's teat. She remembered the simple joy of being loved, her mother's heartbeat close to her ears whilst she fed.

The unnatural equipment above Willow was nearly silent to her now. The beating of her heart was stronger than anything man could conjure. Willow closed her eyes in the sweet surrender of the music created by her heart. Willow hoped the rest of the warren could hear the same song.

THE SOUNDS OF SPRING
Janet Wilkinson

The sounds of spring changed dramatically and
the impermanence of the planet became acutely
apparent when coronavirus invaded the globe.

Bird song sounded sweeter being loud and clear.
Babbling brooks soothed troubled minds and the
pattering of raindrops was music to our ears.

Animals roamed about freely in towns and cities
enjoying their own shout out. Even a goose in
York station brought laughter to the nation.

Spring led to summer as we longed for the day our
voices could rejoined the chorus. Mother Earth was
crying out for us to make environmental changes.

With diverse conservation projects taking place
throughout the world relationships between man
and nature are beginning to pay dividends.

Yet nature still plagues us with many challenges.
Earthquakes, volcanoes, wild fires, storms, floods
are disasters we have become accustomed to.

But, Coronavirus was an unseen danger that took
us by surprise filling our hearts and minds with dread.
Ordered indoors we hunkered down for the duration.

Now that science has now produced a vaccine we
hope that many more of us will hear the beautiful
sounds when spring comes around next year.

PRECIPITATION
Janet Wilkinson

I love that rain has many guises.
Drizzle, downpour, deluge, hail,
torrent and shower to name a few.

Spring showers delight as they bounce
off the ground promising to bring forth
an abundance of beautiful flowers.

Summer rain cools the warmth of the day
and rainbows always appear in the heavens
above when sunshine and raindrops mingle.

Cold autumn rain is best watched from
indoors as raindrops roll haphazardly down
window panes to the delight of little children.

Rain is harsh when winter storms gather.
Violent winds blow sleet and snow over
the landscape forcing many to stay inside.

A hidden bonus comes with every fall of rain.
Electrically charged ions contained within
the raindrops are very good for our brains.

So it may be best to leave your hat at home
when you go out walking in the rain

WILDFIRE

Rachel Meade

Looking back, Ruth's frustration on the journey from Rhodes airport will feel trivial, but now her face burns as she struggles with the coach's broken blind. The air conditioning flounders in the 40 degree heat. As the coach hugs coast roads, she imagines herself the fulcrum between the bay on one side and forested hills rising to the other. She feels she might tip at any point.

"Mummy, it says we need to plant 200 trees to offset the carbon from our flights" Flora looks up from her phone with wrinkled brows. Ruth touches her daughter's hand.

"We haven't flown for four years" Ruth can hear her own doubt. "You need to travel and you are going to love sailing. Perhaps we can sail our way here next time."

Flora rolls her eyes and turns her attention to a nonchalant teenage girl in front. The older girl's face contorts in a coughing fit, and Ruth feels Flora's fingers ball up. She presses her lips to Flora's cheek.

In 2020, she vowed never to inhale recycled plane air again, an environmental reset in exchange for safe passage through the pandemic. But, as weeks rolled into months, her daughter's skin took on a milky pallor and repeated bouts of covid imprinted themselves like sooty thumbprints under her eyes. Flora creeps into her mother's bed each night. Ruth kicks at the heavy duvet, even as she strokes her child's soft back.

As the coach rattles down the busy highway, Ruth remembers the other side of lockdown: the quiet roads, the warm soil as she showed Flora how to plant seeds, the pungent scent of the first tomato shoots. She remembers Flora poking woodlice from a rotting log to explain ecosystems.

As they step down from the coach at the hotel, Ruth's instability persists, Emerald grass, sapphire sea and alabaster buildings jar against the arid backdrop. Ruth is grateful for the sugar hit of orange juice offered by the hotel manager, Georgios. "We grow the oranges on those hills" he tells them.

Suitcases deposited, they head towards the sparkling sea, called by the jangle of dinghies' rigging. Ruth turns her face to the breeze, tasting salt and breathing pine-scented air. A brown-legged gaggle of children trip towards the thatched beach bar. Their instructor, his ruddy face daubed with warpaint stripes of zinc, waves, "ahoy there!" Ruth bangs her hip against her daughter's. "Come on, let's get you joining in."

Each day, Ruth watches Flora's group in their blue-sailed dinghies flit like dragonflies across the bay. The instructor, Ralph, says Flora is a natural. Ruth lounges on the beach until the heat is unbearable, then lets waves lull her.

Late afternoon, the children return, splashing and tumbling like dolphins.

Two girls have opted Flora into their pod. "Mum, mind if I.." Flora races off without glancing back. Ruth savours the sunset's glow reflected in her wineglass.

On day six Ruth is awakened, disoriented, from her doze by the screech of birds flocking out overhead. Dark clouds are gathering. The sea is scarlet like sunset, but Flora's little fleet of boats is still far out towards horizon. Then she smells the smoke.

"Wildfire! Get to the shoreline now" commands the manager, Georgios. The languid bodies around the pool erupt into a confused frenzy as if a wasps nest has been poked. The hum of voices buzzes in Ruth's ears.

Guests swarm towards the beach bar and Ruth stumbles in the sand as she tries to follow them.

"Up, up. We must evacuate to the next bay." Georgios ushers her urgently forward.

Hotel staff marshal guests into boats.

Ruth cannot inhale. She covers her mouth with her dress but smoke sticks in her throat. Later she will recall pine scent amongst the acrid haze. Through streaming eyes, she spots the sails of Flora's fleet. The dinghies are sailing towards shore.

"No!" She's screaming now, beating her arms in the smog. She gasps for air, coughs, spits vomit and phlegm.

Ribs hum into the bay, but still the little dinghies approach. Ralph's voice carries across the din "Grab the scuba masks". Ruth heaves the equipment trunk to the shoreline. The dinghies are close, but the children indistinguishable in their helmets. Ralph wades towards her, grabbing the trunk.

"Mummy, here". Flora extends her hand, hauling Ruth aboard. Flora steers towards the next bay. Behind them, the beach bar burst into flames.

They are installed for the night in an unfamiliar hotel, lined up like corpses in a morgue on the cold floor tiles. Sleepless, they grasp wisps of information. The fire burns on. Ralph, in his mask, returned to the blazing hotel four times to rescue remaining guests. 15 people are rumoured dead. Someone whispers it's arson, designed to circumvent planning restrictions. Another tells of firefighters feeding water to blackened wild hares. Flora asks what happens to the tortoises who can't outrun the flames: Ruth has no answer.

On the journey home, Ruth watches Flora surveying the burnt charcoal skeleton of the forest, sees her lips move as she silently tallies the number of trees to be replanted. Mother and daughter do not speak. Ruth's voice will take weeks to return. Flora strokes her mother's hand and helps with her bags.
In the coming weeks, Ruth is racked by night coughs. Flora leaves her own room to climb under the duvet and stroke her mother's back.

NIGHT WALK

Rachel Henson

My boots protest. Each attempt to prise them from the mud grows harder. Each foot becomes heavier as the night wears on. Thorns tangle in my bird's nest hair. Torch beams light up low branches far too late to do anything about them. Head torches are a wonderful invention but attract the insect army of Borneo to my face: a high-pitched chorus of incoming missiles in miniature. Defenceless against the invasion, I give up, wrapping the strap around my wrist. My ever-growing collection of invertebrate friends follow in hot pursuit as I walk into the swinging shaft of light I've created.

I crash into my friend's back as she halts without warning. Wrists angled upwards, we illuminate the branches, peering into the blackness. We are searching for eyes that shine. A glisten makes us gasp. Our torch beams meet on the same leaf. Slanting down towards us, damp and thick. It looks vacant except for two dainty sparkles hunkered down tight and unblinking. In the soft glow the leaf comes to life, and eight translucent legs scuttle towards the tree trunk that would surely harbour more than just that one spider.

We crane our necks to look up into the blackness, interrupting our stillness only to occasionally swat at insects with vampire tendencies. Mosquitoes aren't the only creatures after our blood, but it's too dark to worry about the leeches. When you're of a nervous disposition, it's best not to think about what's eating you while it's happening. There will be time for that later.

Our purpose is to survey slow lorises. But they are hard to spot, often with just two tiny eyes on show among the leaves. They could be a few meters above the forest floor, or far up in the canopy. The only giveaways are the little reflectors in their eyes. Tarsiers are even harder to find, as their eyes don't shine. They lack the thin reflective layer found in most nocturnal animals that directs light back to ours: the tapetum lucidum. Spotting a small ball of fur in the dark is not impossible, but it sure is hard.

We move forwards gently, so as not to disturb the inhabitants, yet not so slowly that we become a sitting banquet. Insistent gangs taunt us with their tinnitus buzzing. They land on my face so lightly that I don't notice their presence until a delicate prickling sensation informs me that I'm dinner. They dip and dance, in and out of the red beam of light leaving my wrist. Red, so as not to damage the eyes of the nocturnal primates we so hope to find.

The forest is not quiet at night. Frogs converse, water drips on plants, and wings provide percussion to the sound of a far-off owl. And there's another, more unnerving sound: the quiet hum of a motor on the river. The nearest village is not close, and I can't think of a good reason for anyone to be out at this hour. Perhaps, like us, they are drawn by an insatiable need to walk in the wild. To stand drenched in sweat and caked with mud at three in the morning looking for lorises. Or maybe they are hunting. It would be best not to find out. The motor retreats from the rainforest orchestra, *diminuendo* in the darkness. The knot that was tying in my chest begins to loosen.

We stop. With her arm outstretched, my friend implores me to be still. Go slowly. Don't say a word. The red light reaches up into the canopy, hitting pale and distant leaves. Two white pinpricks reflect back at us. I *will* my eyes to zoom in and focus, to see just a little more clearly. It's no wildlife documentary. I can barely make out the rounded form, but we've found one. Head tilted in careful consideration, the loris peers down at us. She makes her decision: we aren't going to become well acquainted. The pinpricks extinguish as she makes off towards a covered branch, where the disappointed aliens would be out of view and no longer a threat.

Despite their name, slow lorises can move quickly when they want to, and this one clearly thinks it's time to get a move on. She ambles her way, arm over arm, foot over foot. Out of sight.

Torches down, notebooks out, we frantically scribble down details of our brief encounter. As we etch our memories in graphite, our hearts lift just a little at knowing that, at least in this forest, these endangered primates are still here.

VAPORISING
Angela McCormack

Although intended to make life better,
They've made the environment more bitter.
As well as damaging people's health,
They're often dropped on the floor in stealth.

Enough dropped each year to cover two football pitches,
You'll find them on streets, in bushes, streams and ditches.
The fluid within them is damaging life,
And in communities they're bringing some strife.

Instead of dropping vapes as litter in sin,
We each need them all to be put in the bin!
But this is where the waste problems begin,
There aren't any vape bins to put them all in!

Vapes come in lots of sizes, colours and tastes,
But they cannot be put in with general wastes!
You can take them back to the big retail shops,
Or go to the tip if it's where you can stop.

There is fluid and battery inside every vape,
Which has caused many needs for a fire escape!
Because when they are crushed, they sometimes explode!
With a much higher risk when there is a big load.

Vapes can also poison the water, land and sky,
And breathing out fumes affects those passing by.
Perhaps make time to do a vape litter pick,
Of course, using gloves and a litter pick stick!

But if you start to take each vape apart,
You will be making a much better start!
Firstly, take the battery back to any large store,
Each battery will help us to save the earth more!

Dispose of the pipette in your normal bin,

But be sure NOT to dump the rest of it in!
Recycle the pods made from glass or plastic,
On mass the difference this makes is fantastic!

If you follow these steps with every vape,
You'll help save the air, water and landscape!
Instead of treating us and animals more meanly,
You'll help to look after the world more cleanly.

You may not see the damage vapes have just begun,
But it will affect your precious daughter and son.
To help reduce litter and carbon footprint,
Use rechargeable vapes and help end this stint!

FAIR TRADE POEM
Peter Redmond

Get the Fair Trade habit;
Think the Fair Trade way
You can make a difference
Every shopping day,
Ask for Fair Trade products
In restaurant or bar.
Always look for Fair Trade
No matter where you are.

Fair Trade helps producers
Build up a sense of pride
They feel independent
You'll feel good inside,
Start by seeking Fair Trade shops
Shop there when you can
Always buy from Fair Trade
Help your fellow man.

Toys and games from India,
Ear rings from Peru.
Hand-carved goods from Kenya
'specially for you.
Trade Fair's fighting poverty
Working with the poor;
Poverty's like an illness
Fair Trade's found the cure.

Printed in Great Britain
by Amazon

39931879R00047